Greg's My Egg!

Greg's My Egg!

For the eggcellent
Tony and David

Copyright ©1992 by Darcia Labrosse.
This paperback edition first published in 2001 by Andersen Press Ltd.
The rights of Darcia Labrosse to be identified as the author and illustrator of this work have been asserted
by her in accordance with the Copyright, Designs and Patents Act, 1988.
First published in Great Britain in 1992 by Andersen Press Ltd., 20 Vauxhall Bridge Road, London SW1V 2SA.
Published in Australia by Random House Australia Pty., 20 Alfred Street, Milsons Point, Sydney, NSW 2061.
All rights reserved. Colour separated in Switzerland by Photolitho AG, Zurich.
Printed and bound in China.

10 9 8 7 6 5 4 3 2 1

British Library Cataloguing in Publication Data available.

ISBN 0 86264 411 9

This book has been printed on acid-free paper

Greg's My Egg!

Written and illustrated by Darcia Labrosse

ANDERSEN PRESS · LONDON

Wool walked into the room with a pillow under his sweater.

"Floppy," he said, "I want a baby."

"You what?" asked Floppy.

"I've just seen Mrs Voleater with her six new kittens. I want one too. They each have a tiny little tail and weeny little toes."

"I know," said Floppy, "they are very sweet."

"I want a little baby," wailed Wool.

"But Wool," said Floppy, "females are the ones who have babies, and besides you're too young. Maybe when you're older you'll be a father."

"Oh, *please* Floppy, *please* can I have a baby?"

Floppy scratched her head worriedly.

"Listen, Wool, you can't just get a baby. They don't grow on trees, you know."

"Just a tiny one, please," begged Wool.
"But you have to buy things for babies," said Floppy. "Like chocolate, toys and always make sure they have plenty to eat."

"And what about when a baby cries?"
"I would comfort it," said Wool. "I want a baby!"
"I've got an idea!" said Floppy. "Before you look after a baby, let's see if you can take care of an egg!"

"Look after an egg!" scoffed Wool. "That's easy."

Floppy painted a little face on an egg and then carefully laid it in Wool's paws.

"Here's your baby," she said. "It's a little boy and he's called Greg."

"Greg's my egg!" giggled Wool.

"A baby is fragile, Wool, like an egg. You have to be careful with it."

Wool took great care of his egg and
shared his favourite toys with him.
   Then he read him a good story.
   "I bet you're hungry, Greggy," said
Wool. "Let's have some peas!"

Later, they played with Wool's toy plane, but Wool forgot about the ejector seat.

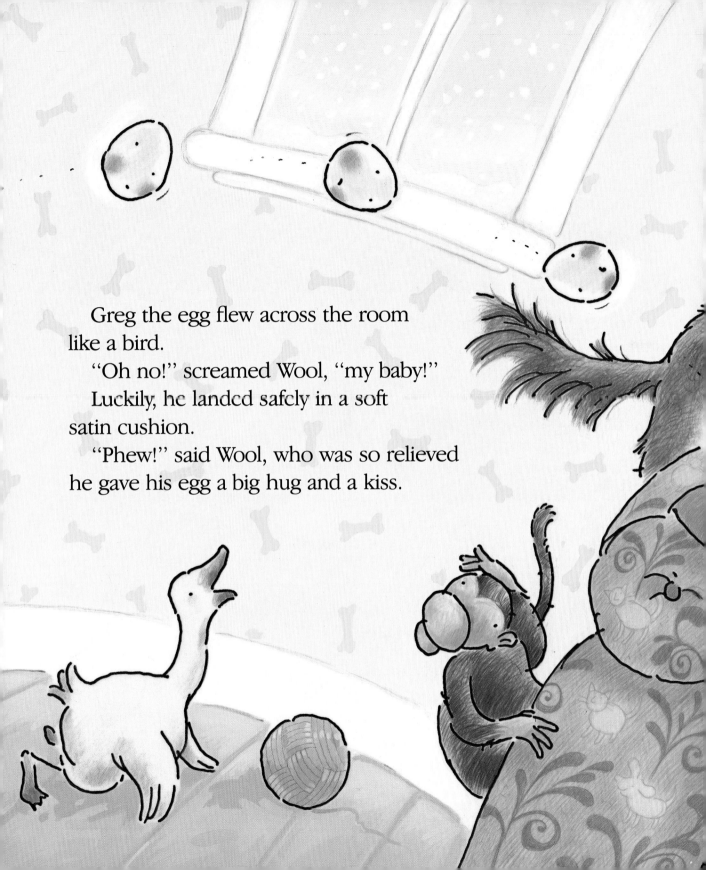

Greg the egg flew across the room like a bird.

"Oh no!" screamed Wool, "my baby!"

Luckily, he landed safely in a soft satin cushion.

"Phew!" said Wool, who was so relieved he gave his egg a big hug and a kiss.

Fresh snow started to fall.

"I'm going outside," said Wool.

"What about your egg?" said Floppy.

Wool had completely forgotten about Greg.

"I'll need something to carry him in so that he doesn't get cold or break," said Wool, and gently he tucked Greg into a basket.

Wool headed towards the park. The Bigbite Brothers,
Brutus, Bill and Bruce, were having a snowball fight.
"Stop! Stop!" cried Wool in a panic, as snowballs
hit him from every side. "You're going to hurt my baby."
The Bigbite Brothers stopped.
"You're not hurt, are you Wool?" asked Brutus.

Wool got up and checked to see if Greg was safe.
The Bigbite Brothers all started to laugh.

"Your little friend is as bald as an egg!" said Bill.

"I'm hungry!" said Brutus.

"Let's make a sandwich!" said Bruce.

"It's not an egg, it's my baby Greg," said Wool.

"Want to help us build a fort?" said the three brothers,
all together in their raspy voices.

"OK," said Wool, but he made a little shelter for Greg first.

They played until sunset.

"It's nearly suppertime," said Brutus. "Listen to my stomach. It's growling!"

Wool waved goodbye to Brutus, Bill and Bruce.

"How was Greg today?" asked Floppy when he got home. Wool's heart sank.

"Pickled mice! I left him in the snow!"

Wool and Floppy ran back to the park and searched everywhere.

"I've lost my egg!" cried Wool. "I've lost my little Greg!"

"We'll find him," replied Floppy.

But finding an egg in the snow is not that simple. It was Floppy's sense of smell which saved Greg.

"He's completely frozen!" said Wool.

"Quickly, we must get home and warm him up," said Floppy.

The next morning, Wool was exhausted.

"Greg shivered all night. I didn't get a wink of sleep," he said.

When he sat down for breakfast, Wool was half asleep and accidentally, he elbowed Greg right off the table.

"Watch out!" yelled Floppy as she caught the egg just in time.

"Do you still want a baby?" asked Floppy.

Wool thought about it for a while.

"A baby would be ten times more work," he said. Floppy nodded.

"Goodbye Greggy-eggy," said Wool, and he put the egg back in its box.

"Well," said Wool, "if I can't have a baby I can always babysit for the Voleater family!"